Bears Make the Best
SCIENCE BUDDIES

written by
CARMEN OLIVER

illustrated by
JEAN CLAUDE

CAPSTONE EDITIONS
a capstone imprint

Bears Make the Best Science Buddies is published by
Capstone Editions, a Capstone imprint
1710 Roe Crest Drive
North Mankato, Minnesota 56003
www.capstonepub.com

Library of Congress Cataloging-in-Publication Data
is available on the Library of Congress website.

ISBN 978-1-68446-083-0 (hardcover)
ISBN 978-1-68446-084-7 (ebook PDF)

Summary: Bears make the best science buddies,
and Bear proves it by helping each group use
the scientific method for its special experiment.

Designer: Lori Bye

Printed and bound in China.
003322

The Scientific Method

1. Observe
2. Make a Hypothesis
3. Experiment
4. Analyze Results

The school year had just begun, and
Adelaide and Bear were looking forward
to their first science lab. But the students
couldn't agree on the first experiment.

"Let's make exploding lava," Theo said.

"The potato clock looks fun," said Rebekah.

"I want to learn how clouds make rain," said Milo.

"What do you think, Bear?" Adelaide asked.

Bear rubbed his belly.

"I agree!" Adelaide said. "The milk and cookie dunk experiment is a great idea. You can't go wrong with milk and cookies!"

"Looks like we will need to take a vote," Mrs. Fitz-Pea announced.

"Your idea will definitely win," Adelaide whispered to Bear. "Everyone loves milk and cookies."

CLOUD IN A JAR

But when everyone voted,
Adelaide's prediction was . . .

. . . incorrect.

"We have a four-way tie," said Mrs. Fitz-Pea.

Adelaide raised her hand. "We should draw sticks to see who gets to pick the experiment. That's what Bear would do."

"Excellent idea, Adelaide," Mrs. Fitz-Pea said.
"Let's head outside."

The class gathered
sticks from the schoolyard.

"Whoever has the shortest stick
will pick our first experiment,"
said Mrs. Fitz-Pea.

Theo's stick was the shortest.

"I want to do all four experiments," he said, surprising everyone.

"Four experiments in one lab?" Mrs. Fitz-Pea said. "That's highly improbable."

"But not impossible—especially with Bear," Adelaide said. "Bears make the best science buddies because . . .

. . . they practice safety first! And whether they're in a classroom or out in the woods, bears have a wild curiosity—just like scientists. They ask all the right questions."

"And to answer those questions, bears use their five senses to observe every sight, sound, smell, taste, and touch. They use this evidence to make their best guesses," Adelaide continued.

"And their pencil-sharp claws are great at recording the results and encouraging you to do the same," Theo added.

Theo continued, "Bears make the best science buddies because they know that every experiment leads to a new discovery."

"That's the best part!" Adelaide said. "They believe in you and will cheer you on with a big ROARRR so you'll keep going."

ROARRR!

"Is there anything this Bear can't do?"
Mrs. Fitz-Pea asked.

Bear answered by roving from station to station, helping the class test out the various science experiments.

"Wow!"

"I never expected that."

"I predicted it!"

"ROARRR!"

At the end of the science lab, Bear and Adelaide looked forward to one last experiment . . .

. . . and it was delicious.

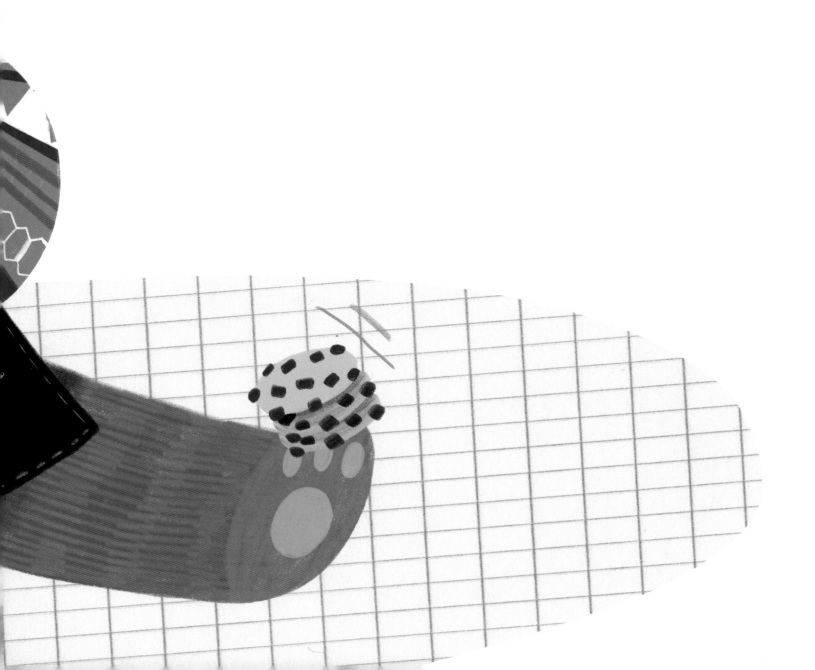

The Great Milk and Cookie Dunk Experiment

What you need:
- a notebook and pencil
- four types of cookies
- 1 cup of milk in a clear glass
- a napkin

What you do:

Step 1 (observe): Observe your cookies. How do they feel? Do some feel lighter than others? Are some thicker than others?

Step 2 (make a hypothesis): Predict which cookies you think will sink and which cookies you think will float.

Step 3 (experiment): Now it's time to dunk! Put your first cookie in the glass. What happens? Take it out and record your findings. Repeat the steps until you've dunked all four types of cookies.

Step 4 (analyze results): What is your conclusion? Did the cookies you thought would sink float? Did anything unexpected happen?